How the Camel Got Its Hump

TALES FROM AROUND THE WORLD

By Justine and Ron Fontes

Illustrated by Keiko Motoyama

A GOLDEN BOOK · NEW YORK

Copyright © 2001 by Random House, Inc. All rights reserved. Published in the United States by Golden Books, an imprint of Random House Children's Books, a division of Random House, Inc., New York. Originally published in 2001 by Golden Books Publishing Company, Inc. GOLDEN BOOKS, A GOLDEN BOOK, A LITTLE GOLDEN BOOK, the G colophon, and the distinctive gold spine are registered trademarks of Random House, Inc.
www.goldenbooks.com
www.randomhouse.com/kids
Educators and librarians, for a variety of teaching tools, visit us at www.randomhouse.com/teachers
Library of Congress Control Number: 00-103426
ISBN: 978-0-307-96019-1
Printed in the United States of America
30 29 28 27 26 25 24 23 22

Welcome! I am Shari Zodd, and I know a thousand and one tales!

Today I will tell you some camel tales, for the camel is a most amazing animal. Every part of its body is just right for life in the hot, cold, windy, and dry, dry, *dry* desert.

But no part of the camel's body is more amazing than its hump! How did the camel get its hump? Listen, and I will tell you.

The great storyteller Aesop says the camel was created by the mighty Greek god Zeus.

One day, Horse asked Zeus for a longer neck, a broader chest, and a built-in saddle.

The next thing Horse knew, why, he'd become a camel! But if you think that would satisfy the camel, you do not know camels.

The Chinese tell a tale of Camel asking the Creator for broad feet for walking on shifting sands, long eyelashes for keeping out wind, and a hump or two for carrying food and water.

The Creator granted all of this. But was the camel happy? No! Because all the other animals laughed at its funny-looking humps.

The camel asked to have its homely humps removed, but this could not be done.

"How can I go on with all the other animals looking down on me?" wailed the camel.

"*You* shall look down on *them*!" thundered
the Creator.

From that day on, camels had such a haughty
look that no animal ever dared laugh at them
again. And camels still have their hairy humps,
which come in handy in the desert, as you will
learn in my next tale.

Long ago, there lived a bandit and his hardworking camel. Day and night they rode over the endless, shifting sands.

They rode in the heat of day . . .

. . . They traveled through the cold of night.
They rode into whirling sandstorms.

Camel's feet became flat from walking. Its
eyelashes grew long from squinting. Its chest and
knees grew furry from resting on the cold ground.

Camel became strong from carrying heavy sacks of food, water, and coins.

But never once did the bandit share his food or water with poor Camel. So Camel learned to do without, except for what it could find in the dry, dry, *dry* desert.

One day, Camel's broad foot bumped a magic lamp that contained a genie! As everyone knows, if you ever find a genie, it will give you three wishes. So the bandit snatched the lamp and asked the genie for 50 bags of wealth and 50 years of health.

Before he could make his third wish, Camel grunted, "I walked us here. I found the lamp. I want a wish!"

"Very well," said the genie. "What do you command?"

Camel said, "I wish the water I carried was for myself."

Instantly, Camel had its hump!

And the bandit had his 50 bags of wealth. But he didn't pay taxes on it. So the bandit was sent to jail, where he was always thirsty, for 50 years.

But a camel is never thirsty—unless it forgets to fill its hump.

But what about the most famous camel-got-its-hump
story, the one by Rudyard Kipling? That story takes
place when the world was so new that there were
only a few animals, including the lazy camel.
During the first three days of the world, the other
animals worked very hard.

Then Horse asked Camel to trot with him. But Camel said, *"Humph!"*

Dog asked Camel to help him fetch and carry. But Camel said, *"Humph!"*

Ox asked Camel to help him plow. But Camel said, *"Humph!"*

The animals begged the Djinn, or Genie, of All
Deserts to do something about the lazy camel.

"He won't trot," said Horse.

"He won't fetch," said Dog.

"He won't plow," said Ox. "He just says,
'Humph!'"

"I'll *humph* him, if you'll kindly wait a minute,"
said the genie. *"Alakazam!"*

To the camel the genie said, "Do you see that? That's your very own 'humph' that you brought on your very own self by not working."

"How can I work with a hump on my back?" the camel humphed.

The genie explained, "You can work three times harder because you can live off your hump." And the camel still works three times harder, because it has never caught up with the three days that it missed at the beginning of the world.

SHIPS OF THE DESERT

A camel's body is perfect for its desert home. Each camel comes with these *sandtastic* features!

The Amazing Hump

A camel's hump is made of fat. This fat can become water inside the camel's body. A well-fed camel's hump is large and firm. A hungry camel's hump shrinks and sags.

One Hump or Two

Arabian camels have one hump. Bactrian camels have two.

Eyes
Long thick lashes keep out sand. Thin eyelids let in light. A camel can walk through sandstorms with its eyes closed!

Ears
Thick hair keeps out blowing sand.

Nose
Nostrils squeeze shut to keep out sand. The nose can take in moisture from the camel's breath.

Knees and chest
Extra-thick skin forms padding for resting on hard ground.

Feet
Wide footpads help the camel walk on shifting sands.

HA-RUMP (camel attitude)

Camels are hardworking, helpful animals. They can also be smelly, and sometimes they spit on or bite their handlers.

Camels often groan when they are being loaded or unloaded, and they are famous for being grouchy. As Rudyard Kipling knew so well: If camels could talk, they would surely say, "Humph!"